For a free color catalog describing Gareth Stevens' list of high-quality books and
multimedia programs, call 1-800-542-2595 (USA) or 1-800-461-9120 (Canada).
Gareth Stevens Publishing's Fax: (414) 225-0377.

The publisher would like to thank Missy Bavlnka for her kind
assistance in locating all of Harry's colorful screwdrivers.

Library of Congress Cataloging-in-Publication Data

Kerr, Bob.
    Mechanical Harry / by Bob Kerr.
      p. cm.
    Summary: Illustrates the laws of motion which had been
formulated by Isaac Newton, the seventeenth-century
English scientist.
    ISBN 0-8368-2248-X (lib. bdg.)
    1. Force and energy—Juvenile literature. 2. Motion—Juvenile
literature. 3. Newton, Isaac, Sir, 1642-1727—Juvenile
literature. [1. Force and energy. 2. Motion. 3. Newton, Isaac,
Sir, 1642-1727.] I. Title.
QC73.4.K45 1998
531'.6—dc21   98-18765

This North American edition first published in 1999 by
Gareth Stevens Publishing
1555 North RiverCenter Drive, Suite 201
Milwaukee, WI 53212 USA

First published in 1996 in New Zealand by Mallinson Rendel Publishers Ltd.
Original © 1996 by Bob Kerr.

Printed in Mexico

1 2 3 4 5 6 7 8 9 03 02 01 00 99

Mechanical HARRY

BOB KERR

FOR ROBIN

Gareth Stevens Publishing
MILWAUKEE

8

10

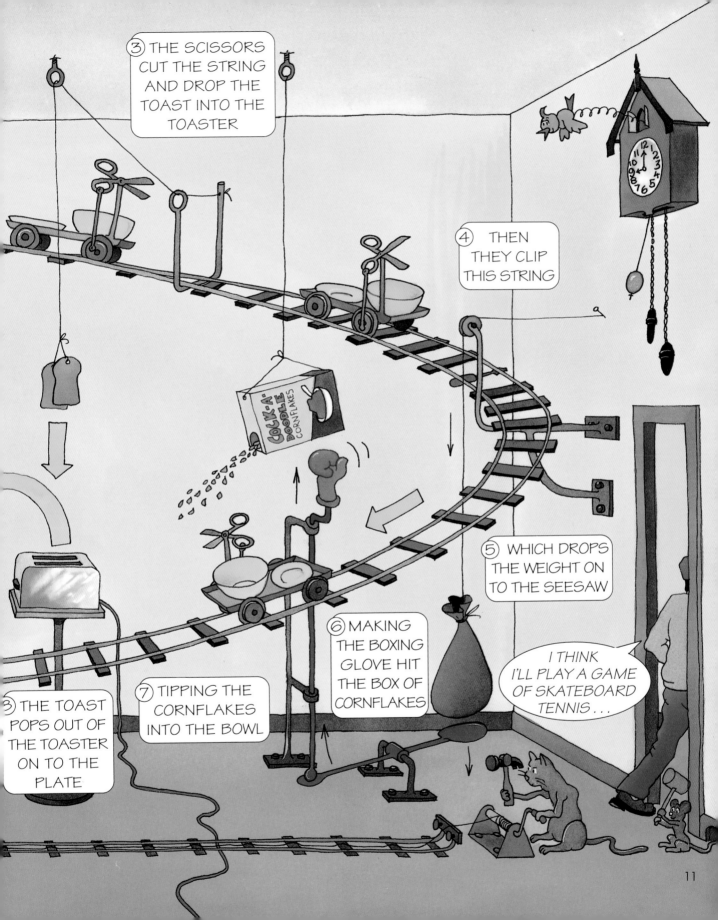

13

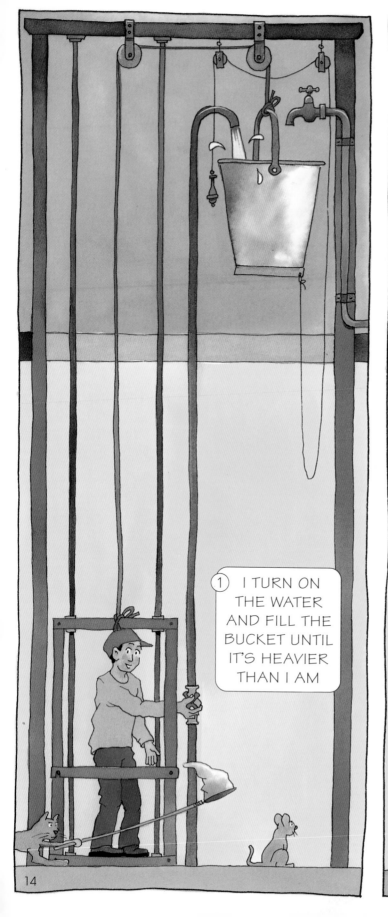

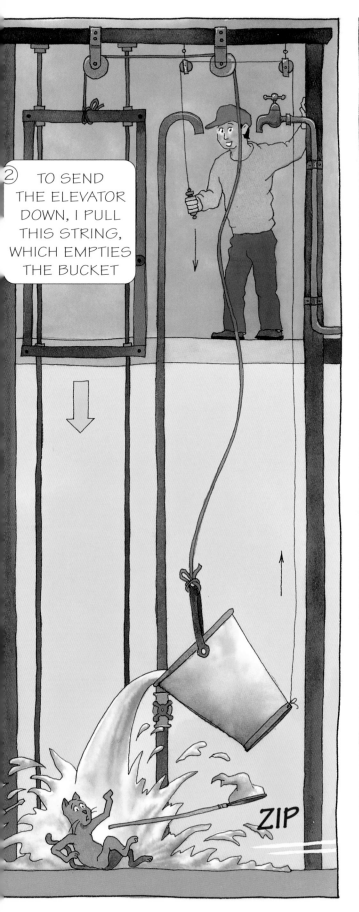

15

17

Harry owns a colorful set of screwdrivers. There is one hidden in every picture.
Can you find them?

ISAAC NEWTON'S
BIG IDEAS
(HIS THREE LAWS OF MOTION)

1 AN OBJECT MOVING IN A STRAIGHT LINE WILL CONTINUE TO MOVE IN A STRAIGHT LINE UNLESS ACTED ON BY A FORCE.

The wagon will keep rolling until it hits the brick wall. (Friction will also slow it down.)

2 A FORCE ACTING ON AN OBJECT MOVES THE OBJECT IN THE DIRECTION OF THE FORCE.

Pushing the wagon will roll it forward.

3 EVERY ACTION HAS AN EQUAL AND OPPOSITE REACTION.

Jumping off the wagon will push it backward.